W9-CNG-135

COVEN

JENNIFER DUGAN

KIT SEATON

putnam

G. P. PUTNAM'S SONS

CALIFORNIA, NOW.

GARRETT, EMMY, & STELLA

4

Garrett

Dead Man's Point, one hour?

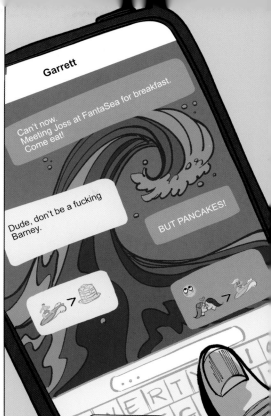

Garrett

Can't now. Meeting Joss at FantaSea for breakfast. Come eat!

Dude, don't be a fucking Barney.

BUT PANCAKES!

Incoming Call:

Joss

HEY, BABE!

5

EMSY, WHY IS GARRETT TEXTING ME THAT I SHOULD BLOW YOU OFF AND GO HANG WITH STELLA?

UHHHH... I DON'T KNOW?

MM-HMM. GO SURF. YOU KNOW YOU WANT TO.

I'LL TELL GARRETT TO PICK YOU UP.

I LOVE YOU, LIKE, SO, SO MUCH.

YOU BETTER.

GARRETT, YOU'RE MY FRIGGIN' HERO.

WHAT'S UP? GARRETT'S GONNA BE HERE IN A SEC.

WHAT'S GOING ON?

EMSY, HONEY, DO YOU REMEMBER BEN?

YEAH, KINDA, AS MUCH AS YOU REMEMBER SOMEONE YOU HAVEN'T SEEN SINCE YOU WERE FOUR.

THERE'S BEEN AN INCIDENT.

OKAY?

HIS FAMILY WAS KILLED. HE WAS THE ONLY SURVIVOR.

THAT'S TERRIBLE!

EMSY, SWEETHEART, WE HAVE TO GO BACK.

I CAN'T. I HAVE THAT PROJECT TO PRESENT WITH STELLA IN TWO DAYS. I'M SURE EVERYONE WILL UNDERSTAND.

IT'S NOT A CHOICE. YOU CAN'T STAY HERE ALONE.

I'M SIXTEEN. I CAN HANDLE A COUPLE DAYS ALONE WHILE YOU'RE AT A FUNERAL.

EM, I DON'T THINK YOU UNDERSTAND. WE'RE NOT GOING BACK FOR THE FUNERAL.

WE'RE GOING BACK TO STAY.

WHAT? **HIS** PARENTS GET IN A CAR ACCIDENT, AND **WE** HAVE TO MOVE BACK?

CAR ACCIDENT?

YOU SAID "ACCIDENT," SO I ASSUMED . . .

I SAID "INCIDENT."

WHAT HAPPENED TO THEM WASN'T AN ACCIDENT.

AND THAT'S WHY WE'RE GOING BACK.

THIS IS RIDICULOUS. I **LIVE** HERE. MY LIFE IS HERE.

AND MAYBE THAT WAS A MISTAKE.

BUT EITHER WAY, OUR COVEN NEEDS US NOW, AND WE **WILL** BE RETURNING.

OUR COVEN? I DON'T HAVE A COVEN!

I HAVE FRIENDS AND SCHOOL AND A NORMAL—

EMSY, WHATEVER KILLED BEN'S FAMILY WASN'T HUMAN.

WE COULD ALL BE IN DANGER. WITH NO COVEN HERE, WE'RE SITTING DUCKS.

CHARLES . . .

WHAT IF IT'S STARTING AGAIN?

IF THERE'S A DEATH WITCH—

NOPE. NOT DOING THIS.

YOU GUYS CAN GO RELIVE YOUR LITTLE **HOCUS POCUS** DAYS WITHOUT ME.

PARLOR TRICKS ASIDE, THAT IS NOT **MY** LIFE.

Garrett: Here!

HEY, NOW. WHAT'S ALL THIS?

LET'S JUST GO. PLEASE.

YEAH. YES. WHATEVER YOU NEED.

EMSY!

DON'T YOU DARE LEAVE THIS HOUSE, YOUNG LADY!

JUST DRIVE.

YOU WANNA TELL ME WHAT'S GOING ON?

NOT REALLY.

MY PARENTS ARE DRAGGING ME BACK TO NEW YORK. LIKE, PERMANENTLY.

WHAT? WHEN?

I TOLD THEM.
I HOPE THAT'S
OKAY.

I THOUGHT IT
WOULD BE EASIER
ON YOU.

NOTHING
ABOUT THIS
IS EASY, BUT
THANK YOU.

IT'S GOING TO BE OKAY. WE'LL FIGURE THIS OUT.

IF THIS IS OUR LAST NIGHT—

FOR NOW.

RIGHT. IF THIS IS OUR LAST NIGHT *FOR NOW*, THEN WE'RE SENDING YOU OFF WITH A BANG.

WHAT?

I CALLED EVERYBODY ALREADY.

BONFIRE ON THE BEACH!

OH, I'M NOT REALLY UP FOR—

SHE MEANS WELL.

I WANTED SOME ALONE TIME WITH YOU TONIGHT.

OH, YOU CAN COUNT ON THAT. I HAVE BIG PLANS FOR YOU LATER.

OH YEAH?

JUST YOU WAIT, EM. NOW, COME ON.

I'M GOING TO FACETIME YOU EVERY DAY.

TWICE A DAY.

I MEAN, IT'S ONLY . . .

SIXTEEN MORE MONTHS UNTIL I'M EIGHTEEN,

AND THEN I CAN GO WHEREVER I WANT.

YOU DON'T THINK THERE'S ANY WAY THEY'LL CHANGE THEIR MIND?

NO, THEY DON'T EVEN CARE. THEY SAY I NEED TO THINK ABOUT OUR . . .

JUST OTHER THINGS.

Messages
You have 72 messages from . . .

Stella
Good luck today!

Garrett
Love you. Text me when you land

Eri
Bon Voyage!

Nikki
Don't forget to text me you b...

COME ON, HONEY. YOU HAVE TO GET MOVING!

SCREW THIS.

WHAT? I'M JUST EMBRACING MY ROLE.

THAT'S WHAT YOU WANTED ME TO DO, RIGHT?

REALLY, EM?

AT LEAST SHE'S PACKED.

BRINNNGG

JOSSELYN! WHAT A NICE SURPRISE! HOW ARE YOU?

YOU MEAN BESIDES BEING MISERABLE THAT MY GIRLFRIEND'S BEING DRAGGED ACROSS THE COUNTRY WITH NO NOTICE? OR . . . ?

RIGHT, WELL, FAMILY EMERGENCIES OFTEN ARE INCONVENIENT. THAT'S WHAT MAKES THEM EMERGENCIES.

EMSY, LOSE THE HAT OR YOUR GIRLFRIEND CAN GO HOME.

BUT WE'RE LEAVING SOON ANYWAY.

EMILY SARAH COVINGTON.

THE HAT. NOW.

I DON'T KNOW HOW LONG I'M GOING TO BE GONE. IT ISN'T FAIR FOR ME TO ASK—

THEN DON'T. BUT I'M NOT GOING ANYWHERE.

WHAT IF YOU MEET SOMEONE?

I WON'T.

PROMISE?

CROSS MY HEART.

I LOVE YOU.

I KNOW.

WE NEED TO HEAD OUT, EMSY. I'M SORRY.

I KNOW THE CIRCUMSTANCES AREN'T THE BEST, BUT THIS REALLY COULD BE A GOOD THING, EMSY.

IT'S GOING TO BE GREAT. TRUST ME. RECONNECTING WITH THE COVEN WILL DO US ALL SOME GOOD. AND YOU'LL LEARN YOUR *ABILITIES* ARE MORE THAN JUST "*PARLOR TRICKS*."

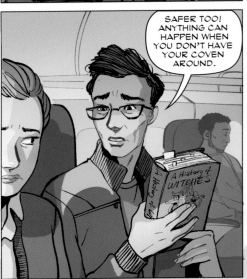

SAFER TOO! ANYTHING CAN HAPPEN WHEN YOU DON'T HAVE YOUR COVEN AROUND.

A History of WITCHES

YOU'LL MAKE NEW FRIENDS. THERE ARE EVEN OTHER KIDS—

HOW'S BEN HOLDING UP?

NOT GOOD. WALKS AROUND LIKE NOTHING HAPPENED.

I THINK HE'S IN SHOCK. MAYBE EMSY COULD—

ANYTHING, PRESTON. WE'RE HERE FOR OUR COVEN. WE WANT TO MAKE THIS RIGHT.

SO IT'S TRUE, THEN? THIS ISN'T JUST A VISIT?

UNFORTUNATELY.

WE'RE STAYING *HERE?*

OF COURSE YOU ARE, DEAR. YOU'RE HOME NOW.

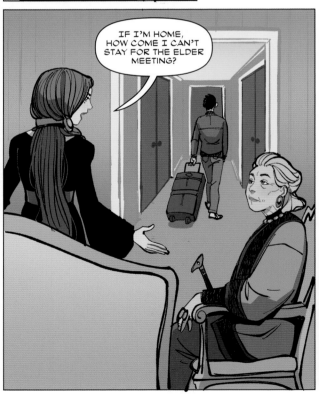

IF I'M HOME, HOW COME I CAN'T STAY FOR THE ELDER MEETING?

SOME THINGS MUST BE EARNED, LITTLE ONE.

GO. CATCH UP WITH YOUR FATHER. THIS HOUSE IS VERY BIG AND VERY STRANGE.

I'D HATE FOR YOU TO GET LOST IN IT.

WHY CAN'T WE STAY IN A HOTEL? YOU KNOW, LIKE NORMAL PEOPLE?

WE AREN'T NORMAL PEOPLE, HONEY. IT'S TIME TO STOP PRETENDING.

AND THAT'S THE BATHROOM . . .

AND THIS IS THE ROOM YOUR MOTHER AND I WILL BE IN . . .

SORRY, I—

SLAM

EMSY, YOU COMING? I HAVE TO GET BACK DOWN THERE.

COMING!

I STILL DON'T SEE WHY WE COULDN'T STAY IN A HOTEL.

YOU'RE MAKING THIS HARDER THAN IT HAS TO BE.

HARDER THAN IT HAS TO BE?

YOU MADE ME LEAVE MY FRIENDS AND MOVE TO A COMMUNE FOR WAYWARD WITCHES—

OR WHATEVER THIS PLACE IS. "HARD" DOESN'T EVEN *BEGIN* TO DESCRIBE IT.

LET'S JUST TRY TO MAKE THE BEST OF IT.

WHY CAN'T I JUST GO BACK AND STAY WITH JOSS?

THIS IS WHERE WE BELONG.

WHY DO WE HAVE TO STAY *HERE*, THOUGH? THIS PLACE GIVES ME THE CREEPS.

IT TAKES SOME GETTING USED TO, SURE, BUT IT'S OUR ANCESTRAL HOME.

IT'S THE MOST WARDED IN DERRYVILLE. WE'LL BE SAFE HERE.

SAFE FROM WHAT EXACTLY? WE HAD NOTHING TO DO WITH WHAT HAPPENED.

YOUR MOTHER IS NEXT IN THE LINE OF SUCCESSION FOR THE GRIMOIRE. WE NEED TO BE MORE AWARE OF—

WHAT DOES THAT MEAN EXACTLY: "NEXT IN LINE"?

IT MEANS THAT SHE'S TASKED WITH GUARDING THE SECRETS AND SPELLS OF OUR COVEN, FOR AS LONG AS WE LIVE.

JUST AS BEN'S FAMILY ONCE WAS.

GREAT. SO FOREVER, THEN?

IF THE UNIVERSE WILLS IT.

BUT PRESTON SAID THERE WAS GOING TO BE ANOTHER SUCCESSION CEREMONY IF WE HADN'T COME BACK.

DOES THAT MEAN MOM COULD STILL HAND THE JOB OFF TO SOMEONE ELSE?

SHE WOULD NEVER DO THAT —NOT AGAIN— AND CERTAINLY NOT WHILE WE'RE UNDER THREAT.

NOT *AGAIN?*

I SHOULDN'T HAVE SAID THAT.

WELL, *SOMEBODY* NEEDS TO TELL ME *SOMETHING* SO I HAVE A FRIGGIN' CLUE ABOUT WHAT'S GOING ON!

IF EVERYTHING HAS TO BE KEPT SUCH A BIG SECRET FROM ME, THEN WHY AM *I EVEN HERE?*

MAYBE YOU'RE RIGHT.

I . . . I AM?

YOUR MOTHER IS NEXT IN THE LINE OF SUCCESSION FOR THE GRIMOIRE, THAT'S TRUE.

BUT SHE WAS ALSO ITS KEEPER ONCE BEFORE.

WHEN WE FOUND OUT WE WERE HAVING YOU, WE MADE A CHOICE.

WE WANTED TO GIVE YOU A GOOD LIFE, AWAY FROM ALL THE TRAINING AND FIGHTING AND—

YOU LEFT.

AND YOUR MOTHER PASSED THE GRIMOIRE ON TO THE NEXT IN LINE.

BEN'S FAMILY.

I HAVE TO GET BACK DOWN THERE. I'LL CHECK IN ON YOU LATER. WE CAN TALK MORE.

IS THAT A PICTURE OF WHAT I THINK IT IS?

IT DEPENDS. DO YOU THINK IT'S A PICTURE OF SOMEONE WHO'S PROBABLY MY ANCESTOR BEING BURNED ALIVE?

SURE?

THEN YES.

OKAY, THAT'S CREEPY AS SHIT. WHEN GARRETT COMES OVER TOMORROW FOR OUR DAILY WE-MISS-EMSY PITY PARTY, I'LL STEAL HIS CAR AND COME KIDNAP YOU.

I DON'T WANT TO, BUT—

THEN SHUT UP. PLEASE. I'D RATHER LOVE AND MISS YOU TO DEATH THAN NOT HAVE YOU AT ALL.

IF I WAS THERE RIGHT NOW . . .

WHAT WOULD WE BE DOING?

KNOCK KNOCK

WELL, FIRST, I WOULD KISS—

LIGHTS OUT, EM. FIRST DAY AT THE NEW SCHOOL TOMORROW. BETTER REST UP!

RIGHT, YEAH, OKAY. NIGHT, DAD. I'M JUST SAYING BYE TO JOSS.

HI, JOSS. BYE, JOSS.

SO, UM, YEAH. WE'LL JUST . . .

PICK THIS UP WHERE WE LEFT OFF ANOTHER TIME?

YES, PLEASE.

SO . . .

CAN WE NOT?

DON'T.

WHY'D YOU OFFER ME A RIDE, THEN?

I DIDN'T. I SAID I WAS LEAVING. YOU FOLLOWED ME TO THE CAR.

THAT'S NOT . . . WHATEVER.

I WASN'T ALLOWED TO DRIVE ALONE.

WHAT?

I NEVER DROVE ALONE BEFORE. MY PARENTS DIDN'T LET ME.

MY SISTER ALWAYS HAD TO COME, OR THEY'D PICK ME UP.

THEY SAID SHE WAS THE RESPONSIBLE ONE, EVEN THOUGH I'M THREE YEARS OLDER.

WAS THREE YEARS OLDER.

I'M SO SORRY FOR WHAT HAPPENED.

WHY? YOU DIDN'T EVEN KNOW US.

WE USED TO PLAY TOGETHER, REMEMBER? WHEN WE WOULD COME BACK TO VISIT?

I HAVEN'T SEEN YOU, OR YOUR PARENTS, IN OVER A DECADE.

AND NOW YOU'RE HERE TO, WHAT, SAVE THE DAY? IF YOUR MOM HADN'T . . .

IF MY MOM HADN'T WHAT? PASSED ON THE—

JUST STAY OUT OF MY WAY, OKAY?

HEY, AS SOON AS I CAN FIND A WAY BACK TO CALI, I'M OUT OF HERE.

THE APPLE DOESN'T FALL FAR FROM THE TREE, I SEE.

EVERYBODY KNOWS EVERYBODY HERE. I CAN'T BELIEVE HE'S BACK . . . AND OFFERING RIDES.

WERE YOU RIDING WITH BEN?

OH . . . UH, YEAH. YOU KNOW HIM?

ARE YOU GUYS FRIENDS, OR . . . ?

I WOULDN'T CALL US FRIENDS. HE CAN BE A LITTLE . . . CRANKY.

SO IT'S NOT JUST ME, THEN?

DEFINITELY NOT. I THINK HIS SISTER AND ASHLEY ARE THE ONLY TWO PEOPLE HE ACTUALLY LIKES. LIKED?

WHO'S ASHLEY? HIS GIRLFRIEND OR SOMETHING?

YEAH, NO. YOU'LL MEET ASHLEY SOON, I'M SURE.

OH, THANK GOD. LUNCH.

Read chapters 3-6
Answer questions on page
Homework due Tuesd...

HEY. EMILY, RIGHT?

EMSY, ACTUALLY.

AH, ANOTHER MEMBER OF THE BAD-FIRST-NAMES CLUB.

I'M ASHLEY, BUT I PREFER ASH.

EMSY, YOU REMEMBER MATT AND ROAN. THIS IS BRYNN.

GUYS, THIS IS EMSY. SHE'S FROM CALIFORNIA. IT'S HER FIRST DAY.

HEY.

SO, WHAT DO YOU THINK OF THE PLACE?

HONESTLY? I MISS MY OLD SCHOOL. I MISS MY FRIENDS. I MISS THE OCEAN. BUT OTHER THAN THAT—

OTHER THAN THAT, MRS. LINCOLN, HOW WAS THE PLAY?

SERIOUSLY, MATT?

WHAT? SHE LAUGHED.

HA! HA! HA!

SO WHERE ARE YOU STAYING? DO YOU ALREADY HAVE A PLACE HERE?

I'M STAYING WITH OUR . . .

WITH THAT KID BEN AND EVERYBODY. FOR NOW.

IT'S ON, UM, MELODY LANE, I THINK?

YOU'RE STAYING AT BEN'S HOUSE?

NOT HIS *HOUSE* HOUSE. NOT WHERE . . .

YOU KNOW . . . HAPPENED. BUT YEAH.

WE'RE STAYING AT THE SAME PLACE. WHY?

IT'S JUST . . . THERE ARE RUMORS.

LIKE?

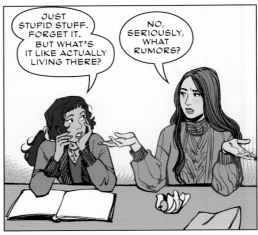

JUST STUPID STUFF. FORGET IT. BUT WHAT'S IT LIKE ACTUALLY LIVING THERE?

NO, SERIOUSLY, WHAT RUMORS?

THERE'VE BEEN STORIES ABOUT SOME OF THE FAMILIES HERE FOR YEARS.

PEOPLE SAY THEY WORSHIP THE DEVIL OR SOMETHING.

BEN'S ONE OF THEM.

AND EVERYBODY WHO LIVES IN THAT PLACE ON MELODY LANE.

DEVIL WORSHIP?

YOU DON'T SERIOUSLY BELIEVE THAT. DO YOU?

I'M SURE WHATEVER HAPPENED TO HIS FAMILY WAS LIKE A BURGLARY GONE BAD OR SOMETHING.

YOU'RE THE ONE WHO HEARD YOUR DAD SAY HIS FAMILY WAS LITERALLY TORN APART!

MATT, WHAT IS WRONG WITH YOU?

I THINK I'M GONNA GO FIND MY NEXT CLASS EARLY.

I CAN SHOW YOU WHERE IT IS.

NO, I'M GOOD.

BUT THANKS.

WHAT ARE YOU THINKING! YOU COULD BURN THIS PLACE DOWN.

I CAN CONTROL MY FLAME... CAN'T YOU?

WHAT IF SOMEONE SAW?

NO ONE WOULD BELIEVE IT ANYWAY.

SO, NOW, HOW ABOUT THAT RIDE?

I THINK BEN'S GIVING ME A RIDE.

BEN HAS CROSS-COUNTRY PRACTICE. HE'S STAYING AFTER.

THEN MAYBE KELSEY.

THAT HURTS.

SORRY, IT'S JUST...

YOUR GIRLFRIEND?

KINDA.

YOU'RE NOT SCARING THIS POOR GIRL, ARE YOU?

YOUR MOM WILL BE BACK SOON, AND I WILL *RAT* YOU OUT IF YOU ARE.

JOLENE! I THOUGHT WE HAD SOMETHING!

SISTERS BEFORE MISTERS.

THE WOMEN OF THIS COVEN ALWAYS COME FIRST.

YOU'RE PART OF IT TOO?

PRESTON AND JULIE OWN THIS RESTAURANT. DIDN'T ASH TELL YOU?

HALF THE STAFF HERE GREW UP WITH YOUR MOTHER.

NO, HE MUST HAVE FORGOTTEN TO MENTION THAT WHEN HE WAS BRIBING ME WITH "BUYING" ME FOOD.

OH, DON'T WORRY. HE'S DEFINITELY GONNA PAY.

I REALLY DO PAY SOMETIMES! OCCASIONALLY!

OKAY, ONLY ONCE, BUT STILL.

UH-HUH. BUT BACK TO THE DEATH-WITCH THING . . .

MY DAD THINKS A DEATH WITCH IS BEHIND ALL OF THIS.

PRESTON SAID SOMETHING ABOUT THAT TOO.

BUT FROM ALL THE READING I'VE DONE, IT SEEMS LIKE DEATH WITCHES ARE A NONISSUE.

HOW COME?

SO THE WITCH WARS, RIGHT?

IT WAS KIND OF LIKE A CIVIL WAR BUT WITH EVERY COVEN AGAINST ONE ANOTHER.

AND THE DEATH WITCHES WERE BEHIND IT ALL, SOWING THEIR CHAOS MAGIC AND CONJURING THINGS THAT LOOKED LIKE PEOPLE.

IT WAS A MESS.

WHY, THOUGH?

THE PREVAILING THEORY IS THAT THEY REALIZED HOW POWERFUL THEY HAD GOTTEN AND BECAME "WITCH SUPREMACISTS" OR WHATEVER.

HI, EMSY.

SHE'S OUR NEW COVENMATE. ANOTHER ELEMENTAL. I BET SHE'D LOVE TO SEE YOU TWO PRACTICE.

I'M BETTER THAN MY BROTHER. EVEN MAMA SAYS SO.

MAMA DOES *NOT* SAY SO. I SAID YOU'RE FASTER AT GETTING THE WATER MOLECULES IN THE AIR TO LISTEN.

THAT DOESN'T MAKE YOU BETTER OR WORSE THAN CARTER, JUST MORE EFFICIENT.

YES, MAMA.

EMSY, IT'S LOVELY TO SEE YOU, BUT THE TWINS HAVE HOMEWORK.

CARTER? MAE? LET'S LEAVE YOUR BROTHER ALONE TO EAT WITH HIS FRIEND.

SPEAKING OF PRACTICING . . .

FINISH EATING, AND LET'S GO.

GO WHERE?

TO PRACTICE OUR CRAFT. OBVIOUSLY. IT'LL BE NICE TO HAVE A SPARRING PARTNER.

I DON'T— I DON'T REALLY DO THAT. ASIDE FROM OCCASIONALLY LIGHTING CANDLES . . .

YOU DON'T PRACTICE?

NO.

LIKE, AT ALL?

AT ALL.

WHY???

I ALMOST BURNED DOWN MY GIRLFRIEND'S HOUSE ONCE.

I PULLED BACK AT THE LAST SECOND, BUT I DON'T DO IT UNLESS MY PARENTS ARE AROUND OR I'M BY WATER.

AND I DON'T SEE ANY OCEANS HERE, SO . . .

NO, NO OCEANS. BUT I KNOW THE NEXT BEST THING.

SO ARE THE COVENS, LIKE, STILL TRACKING THE EXILED DEATH WITCHES? TO MAKE SURE THEY DON'T COME BACK?

PROBABLY? THAT'S NOT EXACTLY SOMETHING THE ELDERS TELL THE COVEN KIDS, SO WHO KNOWS?

BUT COME ON, ENOUGH HISTORY. LET'S GO PLAY WITH FIRE.

HARRISON'S POND

ARE YOU SURE YOU KNOW WHAT YOU'RE DOING?

DOES ANYONE?

THAT'S NOT REASSURING!

IT WASN'T MEANT TO BE. NOW GET IN HERE.

I DON'T KNOW IF THIS IS A GOOD IDEA.

YOU HAVE TO PRACTICE. IF LISEL FINDS OUT YOU HAVEN'T BEEN—

WHO'S GONNA TELL HER?

YOU HAVE TO BE ABLE TO PROTECT YOURSELF. ESPECIALLY WITH EVERYTHING GOING ON.

PROTECT MYSELF FROM WHAT?!

YOU BASICALLY SAID DEATH WITCHES DON'T EXIST ANYMORE. AND NOW SUDDENLY IT'S LIFE-AND-DEATH JUST BECAUSE YOU WANT SOMEONE TO PLAY WITH?

RIGHT. I'M GOING HOME.

JUST BECAUSE IT WASN'T A DEATH WITCH DOESN'T MEAN IT WASN'T A WITCH AT ALL!

I JUST WANT YOU TO BE SAFE.

YOU NEED WATER? THERE'S WATER. YOU DON'T WANT ANYONE TO SEE? THERE'S NO ONE AROUND.

THE COVEN ISN'T YOUR FAMILY? FINE. BUT YOUR PARENTS ARE, AND THEY COULD BE IN DANGER NOW TOO.

SO WHAT'S NEXT, EMSY? WHAT'S YOUR NEXT EXCUSE FOR BEING SCARED OF WHAT YOU ARE?

I AM NOT SCARED OF IT!

THEN WHAT IS IT?

I'M SCARED OF HOW MUCH I LIKE IT.

THAT WAS—

BULLSHIT? CRUEL?

WHERE DID YOU COME FROM?

I SAW YOUR CAR WHEN I WAS DRIVING. I WAS COMING TO FIND YOU,

AND THEN I SENSED PAIN.

I THOUGHT SOMETHING ELSE . . .

I DIDN'T EXPECT TO FIND THE TWO OF YOU BURNING ANIMALS FOR SPORT.

ARE YOU A . . . A SPIRIT WITCH? THAT MEANS YOU CAN SAVE THINGS, RIGHT? ASH WAS TELLING ME—

NO, IT DOESN'T, AND NO, I'M NOT ONE.

WHAT ARE YOU, THEN?

USELESS. MOSTLY.

DAMMIT!

BEN'S RIGHT. I WAS SHOWING OFF. I WAS SO HAPPY TO FINALLY HAVE ANOTHER FIRE ELEMENTAL HERE.

IT WAS MY FAULT.

NO, I GOADED YOU INTO IT.

I DIDN'T EVEN THINK ABOUT THE THINGS LIVING *IN* THE POND. BUT IT'S USUALLY NOT LIKE . . .

THAT WAS A LOT STRONGER THAN I'VE EVER FELT IT.

WELCOME TO THE COVEN, EMSY. OUR POWER IS YOUR POWER TOO NOW.

DAY ONE IN A NEW PLACE WITH NEW FRIENDS AND YOU SET A FROG ON FIRE?

NOT ON PURPOSE!

ALSO, LIKE TODAY COULDN'T GET ANY SHITTIER, I SOMEHOW HAVE A TON OF HOMEWORK EVEN THOUGH IT'S MY FIRST DAY.

I'M SORRY, BABY. I WOULD HELP IF I COULD.

DID YOU AT LEAST FIND OUT ANYTHING THAT MIGHT HELP GET YOU BACK HOME?

YOU DON'T WANT TO KNOW.

TRY ME.

LET'S JUST SAY TODAY WAS A CRASH COURSE IN WITCH HISTORY.

AND IT'S MORE BLOOD AND BACKSTABBING THAN FUN AND GAMES.

YIKES.

YEAH.

ARE EITHER OF YOU GOING TO TELL ME WHAT YOU'RE FLIPPING OUT ABOUT?

EVERYTHING'S FINE, EMSY.

THEN WHY IS DAD FRANTICALLY READING PROTECTION SPELLS?

JUST BRUSHING UP ON OUR HISTORY. NOTHING FOR YOU TO WORRY ABOUT.

FWUMP

YOU FOCUS ON SETTLING IN. LET US WORRY ABOUT KEEPING YOU SAFE.

IF YOU WANTED ME TO BE SAFE, YOU SHOULD HAVE LET ME STAY IN CALIFORNIA.

OUR COVEN IS SMALL. IT NEEDS EVERY ONE OF US TO BE READY FOR—

THEN STOP KEEPING SECRETS FROM ME!

THE GIRL IS RIGHT.

SEE?

YOUR PARENTS ARE RIGHT TOO.

THERE ARE THINGS SHE SHOULD KNOW, AND THINGS SHE HASN'T EARNED THE RIGHT TO KNOW.

BUT REGARDLESS, SHE DOES NEED TO LEARN HOW TO BE USEFUL.

KATIA IS BACK. THE CHILDREN WILL STAY HOME FROM SCHOOL TODAY TO TRAIN WITH HER.

LISEL, IS THIS A GOOD IDEA?

IT'S BETTER THAN HAVING THEM SCALDING FROGS IN THE FOREST. RIGHT, EMSY?

LET'S LEAVE HER TO HER BREAKFAST. KATIA HAS NEWS.

FINE. IF YOU DON'T WANT TO TELL ME WHAT'S REALLY GOING ON, I'LL FIND OUT MYSELF.

BEN?

DON'T SAY I DON'T CARE. I DO. MORE THAN ANYTHING.

BUT IF I LET MYSELF FEEL . . . I'LL DROWN IN IT. AND I'LL NEVER—

DON'T GET TOO EXCITED. I STILL HATE YOU.

I STILL HATE YOU TOO.

OH, GREAT, LISEL, ANOTHER GENERATION OF EMOTIONALLY CONSTIPATED WITCHES.

JUST WHAT THIS COVEN NEEDS.

YOU'RE OUR NEW ELEMENTAL?

WHAT ARE YOU DOING?

A BIT WILD, BUT WE CAN WORK WITH IT.

YOUR MOTHER SHOULD HAVE TAUGHT YOU BETTER.

ENOUGH, KAT.

DON'T WORRY, LITTLE ONE. AUNTIE KAT IS HERE TO TEACH YOU NOW. EVERYTHING WILL BE OKAY.

AUNT KAT? MOM, YOU SAID AUNT KAT DIED.

OH, I HAVE. MANY, MANY TIMES.

GET READY. NO SCHOOL FOR YOU TODAY. IT'S TIME TO TRAIN.

THE OTHER CHILDREN WILL JOIN US AS WELL.

WITH ANY LUCK, THEY'RE ALREADY THERE.

WAS SHE SERIOUS? SHE CAME BACK FROM THE DEAD?

I'VE HEARD STORIES. I DIDN'T THINK THEY WERE TRUE.

IF THERE'S SOMETHING YOU WANT TO KNOW, JUST ASK.

WERE YOU REALLY DEAD?

YES. MORE THAN ONCE.

THEN HOW ARE YOU HERE? AND IF IT'S POSSIBLE, WHY HASN'T . . . ?

WHY HASN'T ANYONE BROUGHT BACK YOUR FAMILY?

YES.

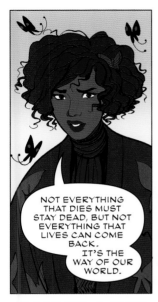

NOT EVERYTHING THAT DIES MUST STAY DEAD, BUT NOT EVERYTHING THAT LIVES CAN COME BACK. IT'S THE WAY OF OUR WORLD.

WHAT'S THAT SUPPOSED TO MEAN?

THERE'S ALWAYS A PRICE FOR THAT KIND OF MAGIC, AND IT'S NOT ONE THAT SHOULD EVER BE PAID.

I DON'T CARE ABOUT THE PRICE.

YOU SHOULD! YOU SHOULD CARE! WHAT YOU GET BACK IS NOT ALWAYS WHAT YOU LOST!

SHH . . . SHH . . . HE'S A CHILD. HE DOESN'T KNOW WHAT HE'S SAYING.

THERE WILL BE A TIME TO REAP, MY DARLINGS, BUT NOT YET. AND NOT HIM.

COME ON, THEN.

OKAY, CHILDREN, WELCOME TO WITCH WARCRAFT 101!

WE'RE HERE TODAY BECAUSE OUR COVEN BELIEVES THE RECENT EVENTS SIGNAL THE START OF ANOTHER BATTLE.

I DISAGREE, BUT APPARENTLY I DON'T GET A VOTE.

GET YOURSELF KILLED ENOUGH TIMES, AND PEOPLE START TO THINK YOU DON'T KNOW WHAT YOU'RE DOING.

THEY'RE WRONG, OF COURSE. BUT IT'S MY JOB, JUST THE SAME, TO MAKE SURE THAT YOU DON'T FOLLOW IN MY FOOTSTEPS.

ONE LIFE IS QUITE ENOUGH FOR ALL OF YOU.

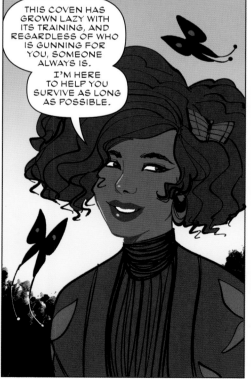

THIS COVEN HAS GROWN LAZY WITH ITS TRAINING, AND REGARDLESS OF WHO IS GUNNING FOR YOU, SOMEONE ALWAYS IS.

I'M HERE TO HELP YOU SURVIVE AS LONG AS POSSIBLE.

CARTER AND MAE, GO INTO THE MEADOW AND SPAR. DON'T HOLD BACK. WE HAVE A HEALER NOW.

I DON'T . . . I'M NOT THAT GOOD.

YOU WILL BE.

BUT—

YOU TWO. IT'S YOUR TURN TO FIGHT NOW.

ARE YOU OUT OF YOUR MIND? I COULD KILL HIM!

SHE DOESN'T HAVE GOOD CONTROL. IT—

AND SHE WON'T GET ANY EITHER, UNLESS SHE WORKS AT IT. NOW, BEGIN, BEFORE I LOSE MY PATIENCE.

I DON'T WANT TO HURT YOU.

I CAN TAKE IT. BESIDES, YOU THINK I'M NOT BLOCKING YOU? I'M NOT THE ONE OUT OF PRACTICE HERE.

OKAY.

I'M SORRY. I CAN'T DO THIS. I WON'T HURT MY FRIEND!

SOMETHING LIKE THAT. IT'S A PRIMER ON ALL THE SHIT WE'RE NOT SUPPOSED TO BE DOING AND HOW TO STOP OTHER PEOPLE FROM DOING IT.

KATIA LEFT IT UNATTENDED LAST NIGHT.

DOESN'T THAT MAKE US PEOPLE WHO NEED TO BE STOPPED?

SKIP THAT CHAPTER. IT'S NOT IMPORTANT.

UH . . .

I SWEAR TO GOD, BEN, IF YOU MAKE ME CONJURE AN ENTRAIL-EATING MINOTAUR, I WILL NEVER *EVER* FORGIVE YOU.

AND I'LL KEEP YOUR CAT.

I PROMISE, NO ENTRAIL-EATING MINOTAURS.

BUT SERIOUSLY, READ IT. DISCREETLY. I NEED TO GET IT BACK BEFORE KATIA KNOWS IT'S GONE.

FOR WHAT?

WHAT ARE YOU EVEN DOING OUT HERE? I THOUGHT YOU'D BE INSIDE WITH MATT AND EVERYBODY ELSE.

MATT'S DOING SOME TEAM-BUILDING THING WITH HIS O LINE. I'M A FOOTBALL WIDOW UNTIL HOMECOMING. GIVES ME MORE TIME TO DRESS-SHOP, THOUGH.

THAT STILL DOESN'T EXPLAIN WHAT YOU'RE DOING OUT HERE.

I WANTED TO MAKE SURE YOU WEREN'T LOST . . . DOES THAT SAY *NECROMANCY*?

HOLY CRAP, IS IT TRUE?

IS WHAT TRUE?

ARE YOU GUYS REALLY DEMON WORSHIPPERS? YOU CAN TELL ME IF THEY ARE.

OR IF YOU ARE.

YOU SHOULD SEE SOME OF MY FAN ART—

OH MY GOD, NO. STOP.

IT'S OKAY. I'M NOT JUDGING.

YOU SHOULD BE JUDGING, THOUGH. LIKE, IT'S *OKAY* TO BE JUDGY ABOUT DEMON WORSHIP.

THE ART OF NECRO

OKAY, I GET IT. NO DEMON WORSHIP. WHAT'S IN THE BOOK, THEN?

I'M LOOKING INTO SOMETHING. IT'S PROBABLY NOTHING.

THIS IS ABOUT BEN'S FAMILY, ISN'T IT?

WHY WOULD YOU THINK THAT?

MY DAD SAID THE CRIME SCENE WAS AN ABSOLUTE NIGHTMARE.

HE CALLED IT "INHUMAN." WAS IT?

HOW WOULD I KNOW?

THAT'S BEN'S FAMILY . . .

I CAN'T BELIEVE YOU WOULD EVEN SAY THAT.

TECHNICALLY, MY DAD SAID IT.

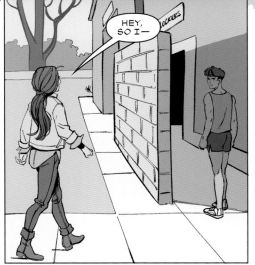

HEY, SO I—

WHAT ARE YOU DOING WITH THEM? THEY DIDN'T SEE OUR BOOK, DID THEY?

KELSEY SAW, LIKE, THE COVER. THAT'S IT. BUT I THINK SHE COULD BE USEFUL.
DID YOU KNOW HER DAD'S THE SHERIFF?

YEAH, I DID. HE PULLED ME OVER FOUR TIMES WHEN I TURNED HER DOWN FOR THE WINTER FORMAL LAST YEAR.
HOW COULD YOU LET HER SEE IT?

IT WAS AN ACCIDENT. BUT COME ON. THINK. SHE'S THE SHERIFF'S KID.

SHE CAN GET US INSIDE INFORMATION.

DON'T YOU WANT TO KNOW WHAT'S GOING ON, IN CASE . . . ?

IN CASE WHAT?

NOTHING.

IN. CASE. WHAT?

IN CASE . . . I DON'T KNOW.

YOU DON'T THINK WE CAN DO THIS, DO YOU?

I DON'T KNOW! WHO KNOWS IF IT'LL WORK, EVEN *WITH* THE BOOK. SOME OF THE STUFF I READ—

I TOLD YOU TO SKIP THAT CHAPTER.

NOT THAT. THE WARNINGS. THERE ARE A LOT OF THEM. LIKE, *A LOT* A LOT.

ARE YOU BACKING OUT?

IS THAT YOU? THE FLOWERS?

BEN, BUDDY, WE GOTTA GET YOU OUT OF HERE BEFORE YOU TURN THIS PLACE INTO A FLORIST SHOP.

HE'S . . . HE'S . . . BLOOMING?

YEAH, HE DOES THAT SOMETIMES. IT'S NOT GREAT WHEN HE DOES IT IN PUBLIC.

I'M SORRY. SHE—

IT'S OKAY, BEN. YOU'RE OKAY.

NO, I'M NOT.

EVERYTHING OKAY? YOU LOOK LIKE YOU'VE SEEN A GHOST.

YEAH, I'M GOOD. WHERE'S MATT?

HE HAD TO GET TO PRACTICE. HE SAID BYE.

OH, WELL, BYE, MATT, I GUESS.

HEY, CAN YOU GIVE ME A RIDE HOME?

ABSOLUTELY, *PARTNER.*

I THOUGHT IF KELSEY COULD FIND OUT WHAT HER DAD KNOWS, WE COULD FIGURE OUT WHAT'S REALLY GOING ON!

YOU CAN'T SOLVE A MURDER ON YOUR OWN, EMSY.

WHY DOES THIS EVEN NEED TO BE SAID?

YOU'RE RIGHT.

THANK YOU! NOW CAN WE GO BACK TO TALKING ABOUT HOW GARRETT BROKE UP WITH—

BRINGING THEM BACK PROBABLY IS BETTER, EVEN IF IT'S CREEPY.

I'VE JUST NEVER WORKED OUTSIDE MY OWN ABILITIES.

WAIT— BRINGING WHO BACK?

BEN'S PARENTS, OBVIOUSLY. WELL, AND HIS SISTER.

HIS *DEAD* PARENTS?

SHH. RELAX, RELAX.

RELAX?!?!

131

HOW'S BEN?

HE'S OKAY. TIRED, MOSTLY. HE TOLD ME ABOUT YOUR "PLAN."

HOW ARE *YOU?* I'M SO SORRY ABOUT—

ARE YOU GOING TO DO IT?

I'M NOT SURE. FROM WHAT I READ TODAY, WORKING OUTSIDE OF THE ELEMENT CLASS YOU'RE BORN IN IS A MAJOR RISK.

I DON'T KNOW WHAT TO DO. IT FEELS WRONG, BUT HE HAS NO ONE.

HE HAS YOU, THIS COVEN . . .

THIS COVEN IS DYING. AND I'M NOT . . . WHAT HE NEEDS RIGHT NOW.

I DON'T KNOW. ONE SECOND, IT SEEMS LIKE THE MOST LOGICAL WAY TO HANDLE IT, AND THE NEXT, I FEEL LIKE IT'D BE A MASSIVE MISTAKE.

AFTER WHAT KATIA SAID—

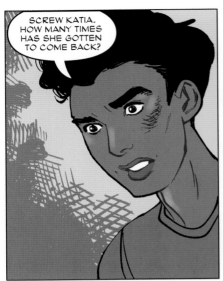

SCREW KATIA. HOW MANY TIMES HAS SHE GOTTEN TO COME BACK?

YOU SERIOUSLY THINK I SHOULD DO IT?

I JUST WANT HIM TO BE OKAY. IF THIS IS WHAT IT TAKES, THEN—

I CAN'T FORCE HER, ASH. IT WON'T WORK IF I DO.

SHE HAS TO BE WILLING, OR THE SPELL WON'T TAKE.

WHY ARE YOU BACK UP?

YOU LEFT. COULDN'T SLEEP.

ALL YOU NEED IS SOMEONE WILLING?

YEAH, AND IF SHE REFUSES . . .

WHY? BECAUSE I'M THE MOST EXPENDABLE?

BECAUSE YOU'RE THE STRONGEST.

BUT SHE HAS NO CONTROL!

I DON'T NEED CONTROL. I NEED POWER.

SHE WAS STRONG EVEN BEFORE THE COVEN BONDS TOOK HOLD, AND NOW SHE'S—

RIGHT HERE. SO IT WOULD BE GREAT IF YOU GUYS STOPPED TALKING ABOUT ME LIKE I WASN'T.

IT'S NOT THAT I DON'T WANT TO. IT'S JUST . . .

DID YOU READ THE CHAPTER ABOUT THE RISKS? LIKE, NOT JUST TO YOUR *PARENTS*, BUT TO US?

I DON'T NEED TO READ IT. I DON'T CARE.

YOU DIDN'T EVEN READ THE—

AND THERE ARE ONLY VERY SPECIFIC DAYS THAT WITCHES LIKE US WOULD EVEN BE ABLE TO DRAW ENOUGH POWER. DARK MOONS?

THE NEXT ONE'S IN LIKE A WEEK. IS THAT EVEN ENOUGH TIME TO . . .

WAIT. WHAT?

IT'S GONE.

WHAT DO YOU MEAN, IT'S GONE?

I MEAN IT'S NOT IN HERE.

IT HAS TO BE HERE. I DON'T UNDERSTAND.

WHO ELSE KNEW YOU HAD IT?

NOBODY, I SWEAR.

THAT'S NOT TRUE. YOU SHOWED KELSEY.

YOU SHOWED *KELSEY*?

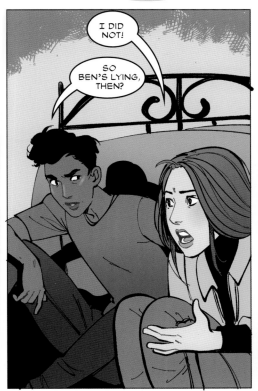

I DID NOT!

SO BEN'S LYING, THEN?

N—NOT EXACTLY. I DIDN'T *SHOW* HER. SHE SNUCK UP ON ME AT LUNCH!

SHIT.

HEY . . . DAD. WHAT'S UP?

I HEARD SHOUTING. IS EVERYTHING OKAY?

DON'T SLAM THE—

BAN!

WHAT'S THAT ALL ABOUT?

NOTHING.

RIGHT, WELL, WHATEVER IT IS, CAN YOU DO IT A LITTLE MORE QUIETLY? YOUR MOTHER'S HAD A LONG DAY WITH KATIA. SHE NEEDS HER REST.

IS SHE OKAY?

YEAH, SWEET PEA. SHE'S FINE.

KATIA *CAN* BE A LOT.

THIS WAS DIFFERENT. SHE WAS HELPING YOUR MOTHER FORM A LINK WITH . . . DOESN'T MATTER. JUST QUIET DOWN, OKAY?

I HATE THIS PLACE.

EMSY!

WHAT?

DO YOU NEED A RIDE?

I'D RATHER TAKE THE BUS.

YOU CAN'T PUNISH ME FOREVER.

SOMEDAY YOU'LL UNDERSTAND. WE HAD TO COME BACK.

YOU TOOK THE BUS?

YOU COULD HAVE TEXTED ME! I WOULD HAVE PICKED YOU UP.

DID YOU TAKE IT?

TAKE WHAT?

LOOK, I'M IN A LOT OF TROUBLE OVER THIS.

IF YOU HAVE IT, JUST GIVE IT BACK.

WHAT ARE YOU TALKING ABOUT?

THAT WENT WELL.

DO YOU BELIEVE HER?

YOU SCARED THE SHIT OUT OF ME!

DO YOU BELIEVE HER?

SHE SEEMED LEGITIMATELY PISSED.

BUT IF SHE DOESN'T HAVE IT, WHO DOES?

THERE WAS ONE OTHER PERSON THERE YESTERDAY.

BUT WHY WOULD MATT TAKE IT?

HOW WOULD HE EVEN GET IT WITHOUT KELSEY NOTICING?

I DON'T KNOW, BUT YOU NEED TO FIND OUT.

YEAH, I GATHERED THAT.

151

CLUNK

GRANOLA

I'M REALLY PISSED AT YOU.

YEAH, THERE'S A LOT OF THAT GOING AROUND.

BUT I'LL HELP YOU—*IF* YOU TELL ME WHAT'S SO IMPORTANT ABOUT THAT BOOK.

WHAT'S GOING ON?

THERE'S BEEN AN INCIDENT.

WHAT INCIDENT? WHAT DOES THAT MEAN?

YOUR MOTHER WAS INJURED. YOU NEED TO COME WITH US IMMEDIATELY.

IS SHE OKAY?

YOU NEED TO COME WITH US.

HOW'S EMSY HOLDING UP? HAS THERE BEEN ANY CHANGE?

NO, SAME AS YESTERDAY. AND EMSY HASN'T LEFT HER MOM'S SIDE.

I DON'T EVEN THINK SHE SLEPT LAST NIGHT.

DO THEY KNOW WHAT HAPPENED?

I'VE HEARD BITS AND PIECES.

HER MOM WAS TRYING TO FORM A PSYCHIC LINK TO THE PERSON WHO HURT MY FAMILY.

LISEL THINKS THAT ALLOWED THEM TO ATTACK HER, BUT KATIA'S NOT SURE. IT COULD BE A SPELL HOLDING HER UNDER.

WHAT DO YOU THINK?

I THINK WE NEED THAT BOOK MORE THAN EVER.

EMSY! OH MY GOD. HOW'S YOUR MOM?

NO CHANGE. DAD'S MAKING ME GO HOME AND GET SOME SLEEP. LIKE THAT'S POSSIBLE.

WELL, WE'RE HERE FOR YOU. WHATEVER YOU NEED.

MY MOTHER HAS BEEN STUCK IN A FUCKING MAGICAL COMA FOR THREE DAYS, BEN. *CAN YOU HEAL HER?*

I . . . I CAN KEEP TRYING. I TRIED ALL DAY YESTERDAY, BUT I THINK I NEED THE BOOK.

THEN WE FIND THE BOOK. AND WE BRING THEM *ALL* BACK . . .

AND THEN WE DESTROY WHOEVER DID THIS TO US.

THEY'LL STOP AFTER A WHILE.

YEAH?

AFTER A FEW MORE DAYS, THE GOSSIP WILL TURN TO PITY.

SOUNDS WORSE.

IT IS.

WILL EMILY COVINGTON PLEASE REPORT TO THE GUIDANCE OFFICE? EMILY COVINGTON TO THE GUIDANCE OFFICE.

MR. GOLDBERG'S GONNA GIVE YOU A PEP TALK. TRY NOT TO PUNCH HIM.

IT'S HARD NOT TO, BUT I BELIEVE IN YOU. I'LL SEE YOU WHEN YOU GET BACK.

BEN . . .

JUST . . . THANKS.

MATT?

EMILY? EMILY, ARE YOU ALL RIGHT?

SORRY, I HAVE TO GO. SORRY.

EMILY!

THEY WERE . . . I ALMOST—

BUT YOU DIDN'T.

ARE YOU OKAY?

NO.

WHAT HAPPENED?

THEY WERE MONSTERS. DIDN'T YOU—

DIDN'T YOU SEE THEM?

I SAW YOU HAVING A PANIC ATTACK.

IT WAS REAL. I KNOW IT WAS REAL.

I SAW THE BOOK, AND WHEN I WAS CHASING IT DOWN, EVERYONE TURNED TO MONSTERS.

IT WAS REAL! IT FELT REAL.

YOU HAVE THE BOOK?

NO, BUT I KNOW WHO DOES. IT'S MATT.

YOU RAN OFF! ARE YOU OKAY?

175

SO, YEAH, I'M NOT AVOIDING YOU. THERE'S JUST BEEN A LOT HAPPENING AND . . .

YOU NEED TO TELL YOUR DAD WHAT'S GOING ON. ALL OF IT.

I CAN'T! HE NEEDS TO FOCUS ON MOM RIGHT NOW. I CAN FIX THIS. BEN AND I CAN FIX THIS.

HOW? *BY BRINGING PEOPLE BACK FROM THE DEAD???* THAT'S WHAT YOU'RE WORRIED ABOUT, ISN'T IT?

IT'S NOT THAT YOU DON'T WANT TO BOTHER YOUR DAD—IT'S THE FACT THAT HE MIGHT STOP YOU.

GOOD GIRL. GIVE HER SOMETHING TO FOLLOW BACK.

FOLLOW BACK?

SHE'S LOST IN THE IN-BETWEEN. I WAS TRYING TO FIND HER, BUT SHE'S TOO FAR OUT. I CAN'T RISK IT.

IS THERE ANYTHING ELSE WE CAN DO?

I CAN TRY. YOUR FATHER DOESN'T LIKE MY IDEA, THOUGH.

I DON'T CARE. IF THERE'S SOMETHING YOU CAN DO, DO IT. HE'S NOT THE ONLY ONE WHO GETS A SAY.

AS YOU WISH.

YOU KNOW WHAT TO DO, LITTLE ONE.

TRAVEL WELL, MY DARLING.

HOW ELSE CAN A SPIRIT BE ACCESSED?

I COULD TEACH YOU, BUT LISEL WOULDN'T LIKE IT.

I DON'T CARE WHAT LISEL LIKES.

I SUPPOSE WE COULD WORK SOMETHING OUT.

I CAN TELL YOU A LOT MORE THAN WHAT'S IN THAT BOOK YOU STOLE . . .

YOU KNEW?

I SUSPECTED.

EM!

WHAT ARE YOU DOING HERE?

WAITING FOR YOU.

WHY?

WE NEED TO TALK.

LATER, OKAY? I NEED TO FIND BEN.

HOW ARE YOU HERE?

I WAS SO WORRIED AFTER WE TALKED . . . AND EVERYTHING WITH YOUR MOM . . .

WE WANTED TO BE HERE.

THANK YOU, BUT PLEASE DON'T WORRY TOO MUCH. EVERYTHING IS GOING TO BE FINE.

I'M GOING TO MAKE SURE OF IT.

HOW ARE YOU, *REALLY*?

I'M FINE.

EMSY, YOUR MOM—

IS ALSO FINE. OR WILL BE, AT LEAST.

WE'RE WORRIED ABOUT YOU, EM. THE STUFF YOU SAID ABOUT BEN'S PARENTS . . .

YOU'RE KIND OF FREAKING US OUT HERE.

COULD YOU KEEP IT DOWN? AND MAYBE STOP TELLING EVERYONE YOU FUCKING MEET WHO WE ARE AND WHAT WE'RE DOING?

YOU TOLD KATIA TOO? WHAT THE FUCK? SHE'S GONNA TELL LISEL!

SHE WON'T. SHE'S IN.

BEN'S ROOM

SHE'S DEFINITELY ON OUR SIDE.

YOU REALLY THINK WE CAN TRUST HER?

I THINK SHE'S OUR BEST SHOT. AND SHE'S ALREADY . . .

JUST THINK ABOUT IT, OKAY?

SHE'S ALREADY WHAT?

SHE'S ALREADY HELPING ME WITH MY MOTHER.

AND SHE SAID SHE'S WILLING TO TEACH US MORE.

WHY, THOUGH?

I DON'T KNOW, AND I DON'T REALLY CARE. BUT WITH KATIA'S HELP, OUR PLAN MIGHT JUST WORK.

I LIKED IT BETTER WHEN IT WAS JUST US.

WHO SAYS IT'S NOT STILL JUST US?

YOU TOLD *EVERYONE!*

NOBODY KNOWS THE SPECIFICS, AND THEY DON'T KNOW ABOUT KATIA.

I DON'T GET IT. MADAME BUTTERFLY NEARLY LOST HER MIND JUST FROM ME *ASKING* ABOUT IT, AND NOW SHE'S GOING TO HELP?

SHE SAID THINGS CHANGED OR WHATEVER.

MAYBE SHE'S JUST GETTING DESPERATE.

YOU REALLY BELIEVE THAT?

LOOK, JUST MEET ME AS SOON AS LISEL AND MY DAD LEAVE FOR THE HOSPITAL IN THE MORNING. OKAY?

WHY? SO I CAN DRIVE YOU AND YOUR FRIENDS AROUND ALL DAY? I THINK I'LL PASS.

NO, SO WE CAN DITCH THEM AND PRETEND TO GO TO SCHOOL.

BECAUSE TOMORROW, WE TRAIN WITH KATIA.

WHEN DID YOU GET SO DEVIOUS?

WE HAVE TO GET HER AWAY FROM HERE.

IT'S MESSING HER UP. IT'S LIKE SHE DOESN'T EVEN CARE WE'RE HERE!

SHE'S NOT LIKE *THEM.*

GOD, DID YOU SEE THAT OTHER KID HERE? HE'S—

HE'S MY FRIEND. SO IF YOU COULD NOT FINISH THAT SENTENCE, IT WOULD BE GREAT.

EMSY . . .

JUST FORGET IT. I'M TIRED.

DON'T SHUT US OUT, PLEASE. WE CAME HERE TO HELP.

SORRY. WE CAME AS SOON AS WE COULD.

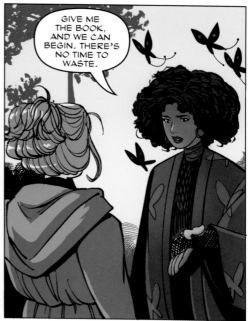

GIVE ME THE BOOK, AND WE CAN BEGIN. THERE'S NO TIME TO WASTE.

THERE'S JUST ONE PROBLEM WITH THAT . . .

WE LOST THE BOOK.

TECHNICALLY, *SHE* LOST THE BOOK, BUT YEAH.

DON'T BE POLITE. BE PROUD. THERE AREN'T MANY OF OUR KIND LEFT.

HERE YOU ARE, EMSY. A BLUNT TOOL FOR A BLUNT ARTIST.

STOP GLARING AND BE GRATEFUL. NORMALLY, ELEMENTALS DON'T GET INVITED TO THIS PARTY, BUT BEN WILL NEED A SECOND AND ASHLEY IS FAR TOO WEAK, SO YOU'LL HAVE TO DO.

IF YOU'VE FINISHED POUTING, TAKE THAT STICK AND DRAW A SPIRAL, STARTING WHERE YOU BOTH STAND.

WHY?

BECAUSE I TOLD YOU TO. CHANNEL YOUR ENERGY INTO IT AS YOU CUT THE GROUND.

WILL THIS REALLY WORK?

IT'S NOT ALL THAT DIFFERENT FROM WHAT YOU ALREADY DO. IT'S JUST BIGGER, LOUDER. IF THEY HEAR YOU, THEY'LL COME.

WHAT ABOUT MY MOTHER?

HAVE FAITH. MY BEST SCOUT IS ON IT.

I NEED TO BE SURE, BEFORE WE GO ANY FURTHER, THAT THIS IS WHAT YOU WANT. THAT YOU AGREE OF YOUR OWN FREE WILL.

I DO. I WANT TO HELP. WHATEVER IT TAKES.

EXCELLENT FIRST ATTEMPT.

OF COURSE, IT WILL TAKE MORE POWER THAN THAT TO BRING YOUR FAMILY BACK.

MORE POWER?

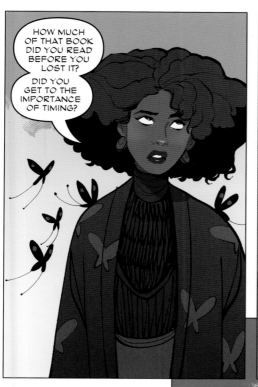

HOW MUCH OF THAT BOOK DID YOU READ BEFORE YOU LOST IT?

DID YOU GET TO THE IMPORTANCE OF TIMING?

IT'S TRUE, THEN? WE NEED THE POWER OF THE DARK MOON TO COMPLETE THE RITUAL?

YES, YOUR POWER WILL BE STRONGEST THEN. WHICH MEANS WE ONLY HAVE A FEW DAYS TO GET YOU READY.

SHALL WE GO AGAIN?

WHAT'S WRONG?

YOUR WRIST—

IT'S LIKE HENNA OR WHATEVER.

THAT DOESN'T LOOK LIKE HENNA.

OKAY, FINE. LESS HENNA, MORE DOODLING ON MYSELF WITH A SHARPIE. WHO CARES?

MATT AND I BROKE UP!

CAN I GETCHA ANYTHING, DOLL?

CAREFUL, THAT'S . . .

HOT.

DID YOU JUST CHUG THAT ENTIRE CUP?

I NEED TO BE AWAKE FOR THIS. TELL ME EVERYTHING.

WE ARGUED. WHEN HE STORMED OUT, I SAW YOUR BOOK. HE DOESN'T KNOW I TOOK IT.

WHEN HE CAME BACK, I TOLD HIM IT WAS OVER AND LEFT. THAT'S WHEN I TEXTED YOU.

WHAT IF HE COMES AFTER ME? WE HAVE TO TELL MY DAD.

NO, YOU CAN'T DO THAT! THERE ARE TOO MANY PEOPLE INVOLVED ALREADY.

I DON'T GET IT. ASH SAID THERE WERE NO OTHERS IN OUR TERRITORY.

THEY WOULD HAVE KNOWN IF MATT WAS A—

A WITCH?

WHAT DID YOU JUST SAY?

GIVE ME A LITTLE CREDIT. IT'S NOT HARD TO MAKE THE LEAP IF YOU HAVE ALL THE FACTS.

WHICH, HELLO? SHERIFF'S DAUGHTER.

WHERE WERE YOU? WE FLEW ALL THE WAY OUT HERE TO BE WITH YOU, AND YOU LEFT!

AND DON'T SAY SCHOOL, BECAUSE THEY CALLED HERE AND I HAD TO COVER FOR YOU!

I DIDN'T ASK YOU TO COME OUT HERE.

WHAT THE FUCK, EMSY? SHE'S JUST WORRIED. WE BOTH ARE. WHY ARE YOU SHUTTING US OUT LIKE THIS?

YOU KNOW WHY.

OH, SO . . . WHAT? WHEN THERE'S NOBODY BETTER, YOU CAN SLUM IT WITH US *HUMANS*.

BUT NOW THAT YOU'VE EMBRACED YOUR INNER GANDALF, WE DON'T RATE ANYMORE?

DID YOU SERIOUSLY JUST SAY "GANDALF"?

IT FITS!

THIS IS WHY I CAN'T TELL YOU STUFF.

THIS ISN'T SOME FANTASY BOOK! IT'S MY LIFE. PEOPLE ARE DYING!

CAN YOU PLEASE JUST *TRY* TO UNDERSTAND WHY I CAN'T SIT HERE AND BABYSIT YOU GUYS RIGHT NOW?

YEAH, I UNDERSTAND. LOUD AND CLEAR.

I'M GONNA GO SEE IF WE CAN CATCH AN EARLIER FLIGHT SO YOU DON'T HAVE TO *BABYSIT* US ANYMORE.

GAR—

NO, IT'S COOL. I GOT IT. SEE YOU AROUND, MAYBE.

COME ON, WAIT.

EMSY, IF YOU COME HOME, I'LL BE RIGHT THERE. BUT I CAN'T BE A PART OF *THIS.*

I DON'T KNOW IF IT'S A PHASE OR WHO YOU REALLY ARE, BUT . . .

DON'T CALL ME UNTIL YOU FIGURE IT OUT.

TAXI'S HERE. LET'S GO.

DON'T LEAVE LIKE THIS . . .

BYE, EMSY.

MAYBE, BUT I USED TO THINK THERE WERE BETTER THINGS TOO.

NOW I DON'T EVEN KNOW.

YOU'LL FIGURE IT OUT.

ANYWAY, I GOT THE BOOK BACK, OBVIOUSLY. MATT DID HAVE IT, AND KELSEY KNOWS WE'RE WITCHES.

WHAT?!

I DIDN'T TELL HER! SHE TOLD ME, ACTUALLY. SHE SAID SHE ALWAYS SUSPECTED.

DO YOU THINK . . . DO YOU THINK MATT'S BEHIND WHAT HAPPENED TO MY FAMILY?

WHAT ABOUT *OUR* PLAN? THAT'S THE NIGHT OF THE DARK MOON.

SIMPLE. WE KEEP AN EYE ON THINGS UNTIL THE DANCE ENDS AND WE KNOW KELSEY IS SAFE.

THEN IT'S SHOWTIME. WE BRING YOUR PARENTS BACK, AND SUDDENLY IT'S NOT JUST OUR PROBLEM ANYMORE.

YOU MAKE IT SOUND EASY.

IT'S OUR ONLY OPTION, REALLY.

SHIT. I'M REALLY GOING TO HOCO, AREN'T I?

I WANT TO TRY THE BUTTERFLY THING AGAIN. LIKE A TRIAL RUN BEFORE THE DARK MOON.

I'M HEADING TO THE HOSPITAL AFTER SCHOOL, BUT I'LL MEET YOU AT THE POND LATER.

Get Ready for HOCO!!

AND DON'T FORGET TO COORDINATE THE CORSAGE WITH KELSEY'S DRESS.

SHE'S BEEN TEXTING ME ABOUT IT NONSTOP.

DON'T REMIND ME.

WHOSE DRESS?

GUESS WHO HAS A DATE FOR HOMECOMING?

SERIOUSLY?

HEY, COOL IT WITH THE SHARPIE, OKAY? YOU HAVE TO WEAR A DRESS TOMORROW.

OH, YEAH. I WAS TRYING SOME NEW DESIGNS. SORRY.

WANT TO HIT UP THE DINER UNTIL MY DAD GETS HOME?

I CAN'T. I PROMISED MY DAD I'D GO WITH HIM TO THE HOSPITAL.

BEN'S TAKING YOU HOME TODAY, AND HE'LL STAY UNTIL YOUR DAD COMES.

STAY SAFE, OKAY?

THAT'S THE PLAN.

I THOUGHT THAT'S WHAT YOU WANTED.

WHERE IS THIS COMING FROM?

I BEGGED YOU BEFORE WE LEFT CALIFORNIA, AND NOW THAT I'M IN THE MIDDLE OF . . .

THE MIDDLE OF WHAT?

JUST, EVERYTHING!

WHY DID YOU WAIT FOR ME TO MAKE A LIFE HERE BEFORE OFFERING MY OLD ONE BACK?

IT'S NOT FAIR!

NO, I—

I CAN'T DEAL WITH THIS.
I JUST . . . I NEED TO SEE MOM.

OKAY, HON, WE DON'T HAVE TO TALK ABOUT THIS NOW.
JUST THINK ABOUT IT. LET'S GO SEE . . .

YOUR MOM.

EMSY . . . WHY . . . ?

WHOA, WHOA, WHOA. HOLD ON, HOLD ON.

WHERE'S BEN?

I WAS HOPING HE WAS WITH YOU, ACTUALLY. HE'S NOT HOME. I SHOULD PROBABLY NEVER TALK TO HIM AGAIN, BUT I CAN'T HELP—

STOP. HE LOVES YOU BACK, BUT I CANNOT EVEN BEGIN TO TELL YOU HOW MUCH THAT DOESN'T MATTER RIGHT NOW. IS YOUR CAR HERE? WE HAVE TO GO!

HE SAID THAT? HE SAID HE LOVED ME?

OH MY GOD! WHERE ARE YOUR KEYS? IF YOU WANT BEN TO LIVE LONG ENOUGH TO TELL YOU THAT HIMSELF, WE HAVE TO GO!

UH, YEAH, I DO ACTUALLY.

COME ON. I CAN FILL YOU IN ON THE WAY.

VRROOMMM

YOU PROMISED ME!

BEN, WE CAN'T BRING THEM BACK. THEY WON'T BE . . . THEY WON'T BE RIGHT. AND NEITHER WILL WE.

I CAN'T DO THIS WITHOUT YOU. YOUR POWER. PLEASE.

I MISS THEM SO MUCH.

I KNOW YOU DO. I KNOW. IF THERE WAS ANYTHING THAT COULD BE DONE . . .

BUT THERE IS.

NO. YOUR FAMILY IS GONE, BEN. AND I AM SO, SO SORRY.

NO. LISEL IS LYING. SHE'S SCARED, AND SHE'S LYING.

SHE'S NOT, BEN. I SWEAR.

KATIA WAS RIGHT: **YOUR FRIENDS WILL HURT YOU THE MOST.**

YOU WERE RIGHT TOO, EMSY. YOU'RE NOT ONE OF US.

YOU'RE BACK!

YOU AND ASH ARE BOTH VERY DRAMATIC.

WHERE WERE YOU? ARE YOU OKAY? BEN, I—

I WAS OUT. I'M FINE. AND I'M OVER IT.

YOU WEREN'T FINE LAST NIGHT.

I'VE HAD TIME TO THINK. YOU'RE RIGHT. BRINGING MY PARENTS BACK WAS ALWAYS JUST A FANTASY. I NEED TO ACCEPT THAT.

JUST LIKE THAT? BUT LAST NIGHT YOU WERE—

WOULD YOU FEEL BETTER IF I CRIED AGAIN?

N—NO . . . THAT'S NOT WHAT I MEANT.

I NEEDED A NIGHT TO DEAL. I TOOK IT. NOW I NEED SLEEP. BIG DANCE TONIGHT, REMEMBER?

BYE, EMSY.

WERE YOU AT KELSEY'S LAST NIGHT?

WHY?

YOUR WRISTS. YOU HAVE THE SAME MARKS. SHE SAID IT WAS SHARPIE, BUT—

SOMETHING LIKE THAT. WE WERE BORED, SO I LET HER PLAY TATTOO ARTIST.

IT'S BEEN A LONG TIME SINCE ANYONE WENT TO A DANCE AROUND HERE.

ONE PICTURE, AND YOU CAN BOTH BE ON YOUR WAY.

HAPPY HOMECOMING?

ARE YOU GOING TO STAND THERE AND WATCH?

OH, NO. I JUST... WONDERED... IF YOU WANTED PUNCH.

WE JUST GOT HERE.

OKAY, I'LL GO.

OVER HERE.

AND GET MY OWN, THEN.

MINUS TEN FOR STEALTH, COVINGTON.

IT'S GONNA BE A LONG NIGHT.

GO GET YOUR PUNCH. I'LL KEEP AN EYE ON THEM.

MATT?

I THOUGHT SHE LOVED ME, YOU KNOW? IT'S BARELY BEEN . . .

UM . . .

SHE WAS ALWAYS OBSESSED WITH HIM. I THOUGHT IT WAS JUST BECAUSE OF ALL THE RUMORS. I DIDN'T THINK SHE REALLY LIKED . . .

HEY, YOU GET YOUR BOOK BACK?

YOU KNEW SHE STOLE IT FROM YOU?

I TOLD HER SHE HAD TO GIVE IT BACK AFTER THAT DAY AT MY LOCKER. IT CREEPED ME OUT. MINOTAURS? SERIOUSLY?

WAIT— WHAT? I THOUGHT *YOU* TOOK IT.

SHE HAD IT THE WHOLE TIME! IT WAS ALL SHE TALKED ABOUT!

I SAID IT WAS ME OR THE BOOK, AND SHE PICKED THE BOOK. BUT I JUST . . .

I LOVE HER. I DON'T—

OH MY GOD. LISEL SAID IT CHANGES YOU. IT MARKS YOU. *THEY'RE* USING THE BOOK!

AND NOW HERE'S SOMETHING TO GET YOUR HEART PUMPING!

WHERE'S BEN? WHERE'D THEY GO?

THEY WERE HERE A SECOND AGO. WHAT HAPPENED?

KELSEY HAD THE BOOK THE WHOLE TIME. BEN'S USING HER SOMEHOW.

BUT SHE'S NOT ONE OF US. HOW COULD—

I DON'T KNOW! BUT WE HAVE TO STOP THEM BEFORE HE DOES SOMETHING THAT HE CAN'T TAKE BACK.

NO . . .
MORE . . .
DEATH.

IT WASN'T IDEAL, BUT WHEN IT BECAME CLEAR THAT YOU WEREN'T COMING TO US FOR HELP, WE HAD NO CHOICE—

WE WILL ALWAYS DO WHAT NEEDS TO BE DONE, NO MATTER HOW DIFFICULT.

I KNEW BEN'S GRIEF WOULD MAKE THE BOOK CALL TO HIM.

I HOPED IT WOULD ALSO CALL TO THE MURDERER ONCE YOU STARTED PLAYING WITH IT.

WHAT IF WE'D GONE THROUGH WITH IT? WHAT IF YOU COULDN'T STOP US OR KELSEY?

THE BOOK'S MAGIC IS BOUND TO KATIA. THERE IS NOTHING YOU COULD DO WITH IT UNLESS SHE LET YOU.

WHAT ABOUT THOSE *THINGS* IN THE WOODS? YOU LET THEM ATTACK US!

IF I'D REALIZED KELSEY WAS ABLE TO CONJURE THEM SO QUICKLY—

YOU KNEW THIS WHOLE TIME?

I KNEW EVERYTHING THE BOOK KNEW, BUT NOT HOW POWERFUL SHE WAS.

WHAT ABOUT KELSEY?

WE'RE KEEPING HER . . . IN BETWEEN . . . RIGHT NOW.

IT'S SAFER WHILE WE FINISH BINDING HER MAGIC.

HOPEFULLY, ONE DAY I CAN WORK WITH HER.

HER POWER IS SPECIAL. IT COULD DO A LOT OF GOOD.

WHAT, LIKE MURDERING FAMILIES? PUTTING PEOPLE INTO COMAS?

CAN I GO NOW?

YES, BUT WE'RE GOING TO HAVE A LONG TALK ABOUT ALL OF THIS IN THE MORNING.

Joss? We need to talk.

I THOUGHT I'D FIND YOU HERE.

WHAT HAPPENED TO "GROUNDED FOR LIFE"?

DAD WAS FEELING MERCIFUL. HE GAVE ME A TWO-HOUR REPRIEVE TO CHECK ON YOU.

THERE'S A PERK, I GUESS. NO FAMILY MEANS NO ONE TO GROUND ME, RIGHT?

YOU STILL HAVE A FAMILY, BEN.

MAYBE YOU SHOULD SHOW ME A FEW MORE TIMES . . .

JUST TO MAKE SURE I REALLY UNDERSTAND.

HI! VERY HAPPY FOR YOU, BUT MAYBE YOU COULD JUST, YOU KNOW, SHOW EACH OTHER LATER? LIKE WHEN I'M BACK UNDER HOUSE ARREST?

I HAVE EXACTLY NINETY-TWO MINUTES OF FREEDOM LEFT, WHICH SHOULD BE JUST ENOUGH TIME FOR THE DINER.

YOU GUYS IN?

AUTHOR ACKNOWLEDGMENTS:

First and foremost, thanks to Kit Seaton, who is the best creative partner I could ever wish for. Thank you to Stephanie Pitts, Jen Klonsky, Matt Phipps, and the entire Penguin Teen and Putnam family, who have worked tirelessly to help bring this book to life despite a global pandemic, a crumbling supply chain, and everything else life threw at us. I am forever grateful. Thanks to Sara Crowe for adopting this book and fighting for it as if she had been here from the start. Thanks to Dennis and to Joe, Brody, Olivia, Bonks, Phinny, and LuLu for being endless sources of love and inspiration. To my family, and to Shannon, Jeff, Rory, Isabel, and Karen for keeping me humble, happy, motivated, and everything in between.

To my readers, and to the bloggers, booktokers, bookstagrammers, and bookstore workers: Thank you for your support. None of this would be possible without you.

ILLUSTRATOR ACKNOWLEDGMENTS:

I'd like to thank the amazing team I worked with on this book: Jenn Dugan, our author, for her enthusiasm and passion for this project; Cecilia Yung and Eileen Savage, whose art direction and technical prowess helped me manage many a speed bump; and our editor, Stephanie Pitts, for her encouragement and thoughtful feedback. I'd also like to shout out my friend Leila del Duca and my family for being the best support system I could ask for while working on this book.

JENNIFER DUGAN is a writer, a geek, and a romantic who writes the kinds of stories she wishes she'd had growing up. She's the author of the young adult novels *Melt With You*, *Some Girls Do*, *Verona Comics*, and *Hot Dog Girl*, which was called "a great, fizzy rom-com" by *Entertainment Weekly* and "one of the best reads of the year, hands down" by *Paste* magazine. She lives in upstate New York with her family, their dog, a strange kitten who enjoys wearing sweaters, and an evil cat who is no doubt planning to take over the world.

You can visit Jennifer at

JLDugan.com

Or follow her on Twitter and Instagram

@JL_Dugan

KIT SEATON has illustrated the graphic novel adaptations of Leigh Bardugo's *Wonder Woman: Warbringer* and Alexandra Bracken's *Brightly Woven*. She is the co-creator of the comics *Norroway* and *Afar*. She lives with her family, which includes a gang of three cats and two poodles, in a grove of live oaks in Savannah, Georgia, a haunted city known for hot sticky summers, the maddening hum of cicadas, and the unpredictable crunch of a palmetto bug underfoot. Kit loves all things spooky, so she feels right at home.

You can visit Kit at

kitseaton.com

Or follow her on Instagram

@kitandcatcomics

To the tiniest frog in the tiniest pond —J.D.

To all students of the arts, practical or esoteric —K.S.

G. P. PUTNAM'S SONS
An imprint of Penguin Random House LLC, New York

First published in the United States of America by G. P. Putnam's Sons,
an imprint of Penguin Random House LLC, 2022

Text copyright © 2022 by Jennifer Dugan
Illustrations copyright © 2022 by Kit Seaton

Penguin supports copyright. Copyright fuels creativity, encourages diverse voices, promotes free speech,
and creates a vibrant culture. Thank you for buying an authorized edition of this book and for complying
with copyright laws by not reproducing, scanning, or distributing any part of it
in any form without permission. You are supporting writers and allowing Penguin
to continue to publish books for every reader.

G. P. Putnam's Sons is a registered trademark of Penguin Random House LLC.
Penguin Books & colophon are registered trademarks of Penguin Books Limited.

Visit us online at penguinrandomhouse.com

Library of Congress Cataloging-in-Publication Data is available.

Manufactured in China

ISBN 9780593112168 (hardcover)
1 3 5 7 9 10 8 6 4 2

ISBN 9780593112182 (paperback)
1 3 5 7 9 10 8 6 4 2

TOPL

Design by Eileen Savage and Cindy De la Cruz | Text set in Atland BB and Serenity

This book is a work of fiction. Any references to historical events, real people,
or real places are used fictitiously. Other names, characters, places, and events
are products of the author's imagination, and any resemblance to actual events or
places or persons, living or dead, is entirely coincidental.

The publisher does not have any control over and does not assume any
responsibility for author or third-party websites or their content.

OCT 1 7 2022